to be (like)

chalk and cheese

- *phrase*. (British & Australian)

1. to be completely different, to have nothing in common

2. total opposites, as in the American equivalent of "night and day"

This is a story
about two quite
different friends. . . .

For Noah ~ YOU ROCK MY WORLD!
Thanks for the inspiration—Daddy x

SIMON & SCHUSTER BOOKS FOR YOUNG READERS
An imprint of Simon & Schuster Children's Publishing Division
1230 Avenue of the Americas, New York, New York 10020
Copyright © 2008 by Tim Warnes
Simon & Schuster Books for Young Readers is a trademark of
Simon & Schuster, Inc.
Book design by Tim Warnes and Lizzy Bromley
The text for this book is set in Grit Primer, with hand
lettering by Tim Warnes.
The illustrations for this book are rendered in watercolor
and pencil.
Manufactured in China
10 9 8 7 6 5 4 3 2 1
Library of Congress Cataloging-in-Publication Data
Warnes, Tim.
Chalk & Cheese / Tim Warnes. — 1st ed.
p. cm.
Summary: A country mouse goes to visit his best friend,
a dog who lives in New York City, and even though
the two of them are very different, they have a great time.
ISBN-13: 978-1-4169-1378-8
ISBN-10: 1-4169-1378-5
[1. Mice - Fiction. 2. Dogs - Fiction. 3. Best friends - Fiction.
4. Friendship - Fiction. 5. Individuality - Fiction.
6. New York (N.Y.) - Fiction.] I. Title.
PZ7. W2483Ch 2008
[E] - dc22
2007018332

Chalk & Cheese

tim warnes

Simon & Schuster Books for Young Readers
New York London Toronto Sydney

Chalk lives in New York City.

His best friend, Cheese, has come to visit.

DAY

We're going to have fun together, aren't we, Chalk—going about the city, seeing new things....

Cheese is an English country mouse.
Even the simplest things excite him.

Chalk brings Cheese to his favorite diner.

Chalk is excited to show Cheese the sights.

Cheese is a little scared of new places.

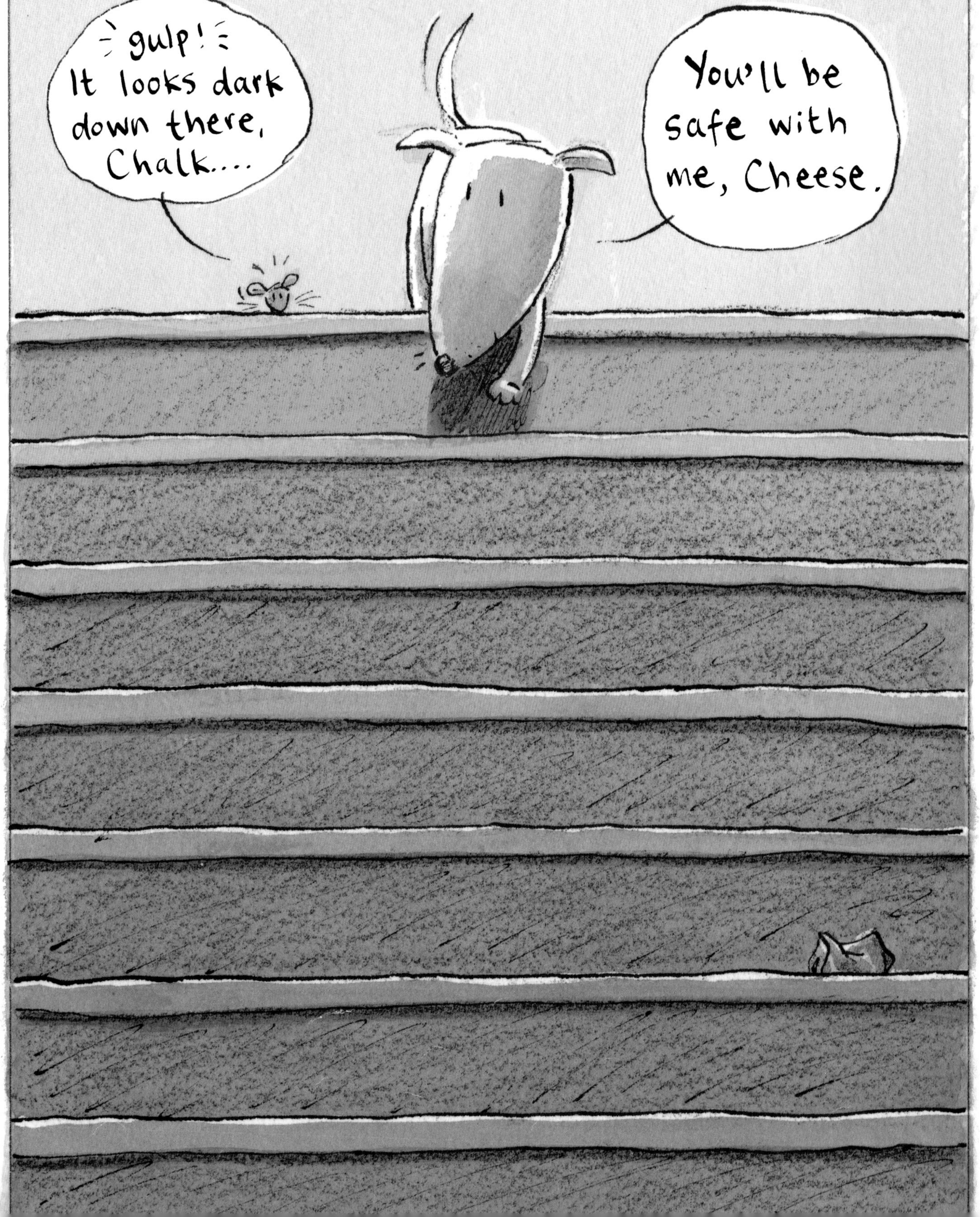

Chalk and Cheese are quite different.

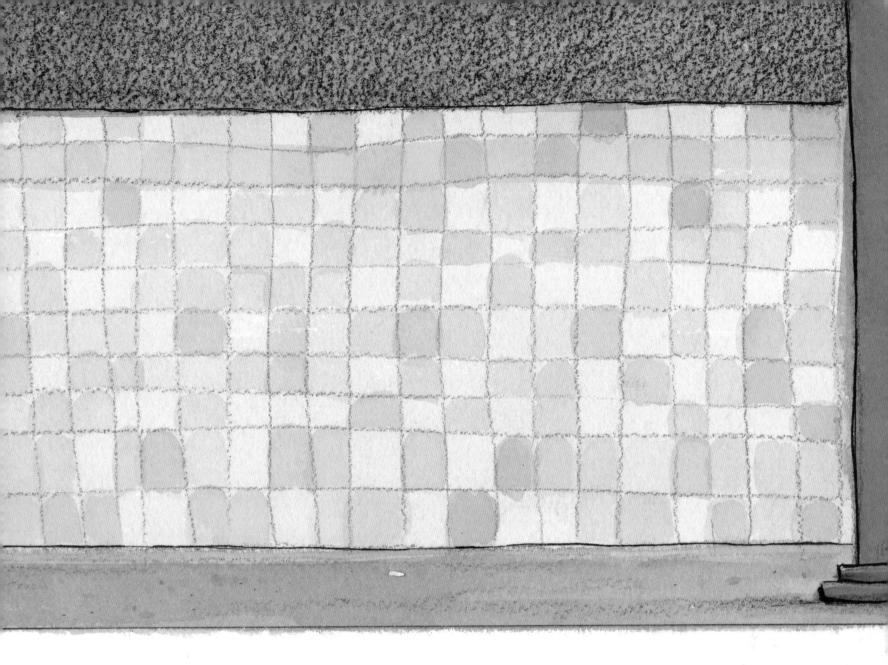

But they are friends just the same.

Chalk likes to admire the view. Cheese does not.

They don't stay long.

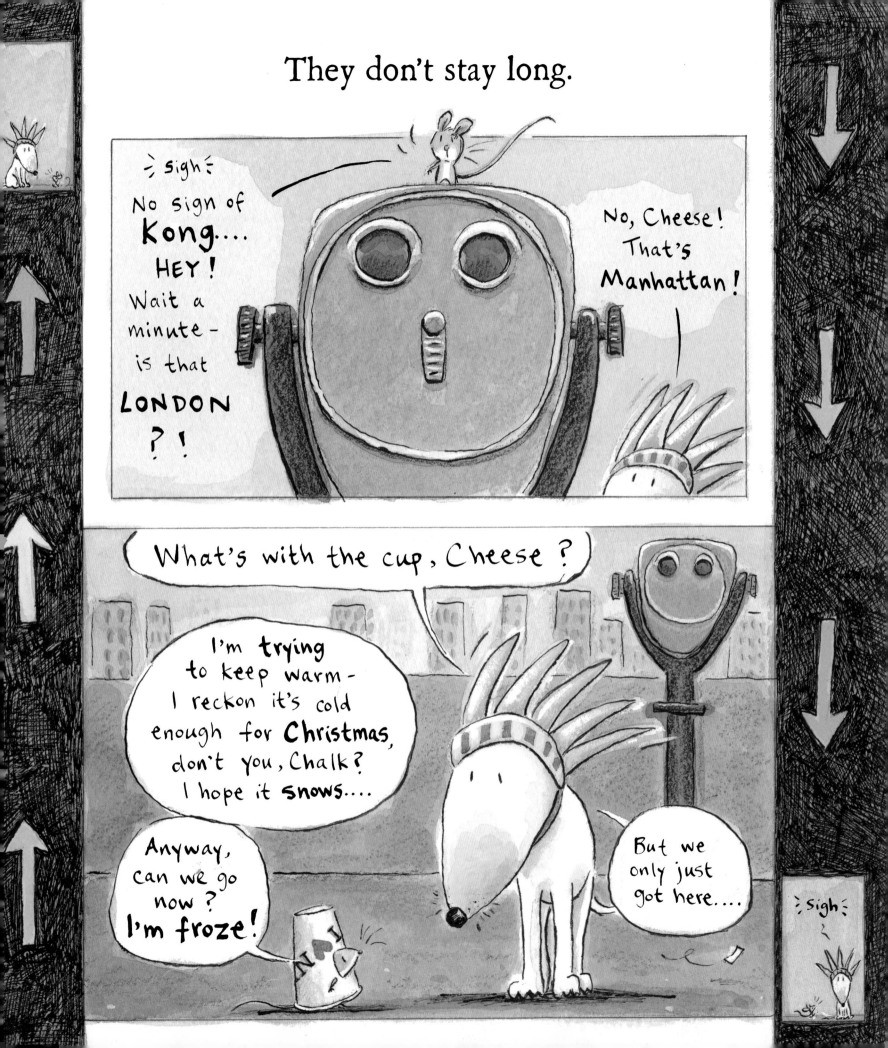

They are quite different.

You might say they go together like chalk and cheese.

Chalk takes Cheese to the Empire State Building.

Chalk and Cheese are the best of friends.
But even best friends argue . . .

Chalk worries too much.

Cheese worries too little.

You might say they go together like chalk and cheese.

Perhaps they're not so different, after all.

Chalk loves Cheese.

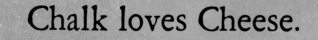

Cheese loves Chalk.

In some ways they're exactly the same.